A day can change your life

For Everyone who has helped
me throughout completing my
book and everyone who enjoy
the book

Chapter 1

The year 2002 a family was living in Afghanistan and in that family a baby girl was born. The parents named her Hena they were living in a part of Kabul city. Hena's parents were fighting each other all the time. When Hena would see her parents fighting each other she would become upset. The time was passing alike. Hena started KG when she was 4 years old and when she turned 7 years old her parents separated from each other. Hena's Father married to someone else and Hena was living with her father and stepmother. Henna's stepmother was very cruel to her and during the time her birth mother died. So, Hena's father took her to her mother's grave, when they were returning home Hena's father was not focused to the traffic light and a car hit Hena.

Hena's father urgently took her to the hospital, she was saved by the doctors and when she recovered from unconsciousness. Hena said to her father, "Who are you and where am I?" Doctors said unfortunately she had lost her memory and would not remember anything. Hena's father was very nervous seeing her like this and was crying.

A few days later Hena was discharged from the hospital and they went back home. As Hena would not remember anything, her father introduced his wife (stepmother) to her and said she is your mother, At night Hena's father got a call from his employer and said he has to come to work urgently. Hena's father had to go to work and as Hena's father's duty location was very far from the city he had to stay there for a long time. So, he left Hena with her stepmother and Hena's father didn't know anything about his wife's thoughts about Hena. Because when Hena's father would be around she would act like very kind person to Hena and he trusted his wife. Hena's father left to work and left Hena alone with her stepmother. Hena's stepmother had very bad thoughts about her. The night passed and Hena didn't know her stepmother's thoughts about her.

By the morning when Hena woke up from the sleep, her stepmother very kindly had said good morning to Hena, kind like her real mother. Hena finished her breakfast and asked her stepmother what time we may go to school? The mother said I am going to give you your clothes and get ready. The mother gave her torn clothes and Hena wore those clothes to her surprise and then her mother gave her a bowl. Hena and her stepmother left the home and Hena was chasing her stepmother because she's walking fast? in surprise and her mind was full of questions. The mother stopped by the place where she wanted, so Hena kindly asked, dear mother why we stopped here? There is no school here and why these torn cloths? Strangest of all what do I do with this bowl.

Henn's stepmother said you will shortly know and sit here. Hena kindly asked why? Stepmother angrily said, don't ask any question, just do what I tell you. Frightened Henna, sat down and the stepmother said put the bowl in front of you. Hena did what her stepmother would say and at the end told Hena by the evening when returning home you must bring 500 Afghani. Hena said how can I find 500 Afghani? The stepmother said I don't know how you may find by begging or anything else, it's your problem not mine. If you don't do what I tell you and don't bring the money, you will find my real anger.

By the end of the day, Hena could not find the money her stepmother forced her to find, Hena didn't have any option except returning home. When Hena got to home her stepmother asked where is the money (500 Afghani). Hena was silent and her mother said didn't you hear what I said. Hena said I couldn't find anything, stepmother said couldn't you find anything. The stepmother beat her a lot and said leave the house, Hena didn't want to leave the house but the stepmother forced her to leave the house. Hena didn't have a choice except to stay out of the house at night, the night passed and it was morning. Henna's stepmother took her this time to a new place, two weeks passed and the mother would take her to a new place each day. Hena spent each night out of the house, after the two weeks Henna's mother took her to a different place. A place where nobody would imagine, the stepmother sold her to some people for lots of money and very bad people.

After 3 days Henna's father returned home and asked his wife where is Henna? The stepmother started crying and said lovely Hena died. Henna's father asked what happened. Stepmother said: she went out and wanted to play, I was in house and after 16 minutes I heard a scream. I went out and saw Hena had fallen from the roof. I took her to the hospital, but when reached the hospital she died. Henna's father cried a lot and said take me to her grave. The stepmother took him to a grave, however it was not Henna's grave. The time Henna's stepmother sold for lots of money, she pay someone to make a fake grave.

Two days later, the group of bad people forced Hena for wrong doings, they were forcing Hena to sell drugs. It was not Hena only, there were many kids the group bought, and one day Hena was crying a boy saw her. The boy came towards Hena and said, why you are crying. Hena said let me alone, the boy said maybe I might be helpful. Hena started talking and told the boy her story what had happened to her, the boy introduced himself and said I am Husain. Husain: maybe we might be able to help each other. We can escape from here and Hena asked why you are here.

Husain: I had a family and my parents loved me and I loved them as well. Husain: One day me and my parents went to the park, we enjoyed that day a lot. By the time we wanted to return home an explosion occurred and I lost my both parents. When I returned home I saw my uncle and uncle's wife, they took our house by force and drove me out of my house.

Husain: I spent the night outside, in the morning I was sitting there and a man asked me, what you are doing here. I told him my whole story; the man said do you want to have a place to live and meal to eat, I said yes and then the man said came with me and you must do whatever I say. I didn't know where he took me, when we got there; they gave me drugs I must sell.

Husain: They oppress us and from that day I couldn't escape. Now we are two and we can escape from here.

Hena: OK and it's a good idea if we can escape from here, but when we will escape from here.

Husain: Tomorrow morning when we woke up from sleep like everyone else, we will go to our daily work, but you may go earlier then me, so nobody doubts on us.

In the morning, Hena went to her work place and Husain was behind her. They saw a person following them. Hena and Husain started running and the guy started running after them. They realized why the guy is following them. Last night when they were planning their escape probably someone hear them.

Hena was ahead and Husain was running behind her, while Hena was running suddenly an explosion occurred and people were screaming and yelling and Husain lost Hena. Husain was searching for Hena and he saw her in an ambulance, Hena's leg was hit. Husain also got on to the ambulance, they guy following them also saw Hena and Husain in the ambulance and wanted to get on to the ambulance, but he missed the ambulance. So, the guy got on to another vehicle and followed the ambulance. When the guy got in to the hospital, he searched all the hospital rooms, but did not find Hena and Husain.

Because, Hena and Husain already had escaped the hospital. They got to the closest police station and told the whole story to the police.

Police: How did you escape the hospital? Husain, By the time we reach the hospital, Hena regain her consciousness. We wanted to escape a doctor saw us and saw the other guy searching for us as well. So, the doctor helped us to escape from the hospital, got us on a Taxi and told us to go to the nearest police station and we are here. We believe police can help us, I am sure you can help us and all other children there.

The Police officer asked us to take him to the place where the other children are. When we reached there no one was there, however the police officer was able to find a piece of a cigarette, half used. The police officer realized the children and bad men might not be very far; the officer continued searching and captured them shortly. The police officer thanked Hena and Husain for the brave work they did. The police officer was willing to take them back to their home. Police: Husain where is your house. Husain: I don't have a house, I can live anywhere. But, not willing to ask my uncle to vacant our house, in addition I am single and they are a family. Police officer: Ok, then let's take Hena to her house. By the time they all reach Hena's house, Hena's father and mother were at home. The officer rings the bell and Hena's step mother opened the door and Hena hide behind the door. The officer: Is your husband home and can I talk to him? Stepmother: called Hena's father and he came to the door. Hena came out from behind the door and Hena's father and stepmother saw her, the stepmother fainted. Hena's father was surprised by seeing her, Hena hugged him. Father: cried with joy and said how my daughter is revived. Hena: I did not die, but was sold to the drug mafia, Hena told the whole story to her father. Father: I don't know what to say. They waited for Hena's stepmother to be conscious. Hena's stepmother got her consciousness and wanted to talk, but Hena's father didn't allow her to talk.

The officer arrested Hena's stepmother and thanked Hena. Hena introduced Husain to her father and after listening to Husain's story, Hena's father asked Husain he can stay with them. Father to Husain: You and Hena can go to school together and be as real friends and Husain accepted his request.

Chapter 2

After two days Hena asked her father, can we go to the hospital and thank the doctor? Hena's father said Ok.

They went to the hospital and Hena's father thanked the doctor and said if it would not be you I would never find my daughter. Hena asked the doctor why you helped us as you didn't know us. Doctor said: I have a daughter of your age and she recovered from cancer. One day she wanted to play with her friends and went to the park. After sometime some guys got into the fight, everyone escaped from the park. My daughter wanted to escape as well but got stuck between these two people. I heard a scream and got to the Park very quickly. Didn't know what happened, just rushed my daughter to the hospital and now she is in coma. Doctor was crying for his daughter, Hena said don't cry we are praying for your daughter's quick recovery. Doctor said I saw my daughter's face in you that day, so tried to help you guys. after few days Hena and Husain started going back to school and they were 4th graders. Hena and Husain life was joyful and very happy.

After sometime Henan's father got a call and was told, they are eligible to migrate to US and they have only two months to make their arrangements. After a week they moved to US and one of Hena's father's friend already rented a house for them. Two years passed and Hena wanted to go on a tour to Afghanistan. The situation in Afghanistan was not good, daily suicides attacks, more people were killed. But, they still went to Afghanistan and after some time they returned back to US due to the bad situation in Afghanistan.

When Hena came back to US, she was thinking about Afghanistan, 6 year passed. Hena and Husain finished their school and started college, after two more years they completed their college.

One day Hena asked her father. What do you want me to be in the future? Hena's father advised her and said I am you father and do listen to my advice. We are from a country where, there is war and bloodshed. Due to the war in Afghanistan all Afghans are moving place to place and we should do a job, that it benefits us, our family and our country. If we don't build our homeland then who will do it for us. You are a smart and sober girl, I don't need to tell you what to do and what not to do. Only focus on whatever you want to do and so far you guys have four years to finish your studies first. You and Husain can think during these coming years.

3 years passed and one night Hena was sleeping and in the morning Hena told her father and Husain:

Last night I was dreaming about you and Hena wanted to tell her dream, suddenly somebody hit the window with a stone. Hena's father tried to see who is it, but someone hit him by a bullet and escaped. Hena took her father to the Hospital, due to serious injures Hena's father had an operation and the Dr told Hena your father is alive but the bullet injury is very serious and you guys have to be very careful him, the wounds may get bad.

Hena's father was released from the Hospital and they all return to home. Hena's neighbor come and asked Hena: how did it happen. Hena told the whole story and the neighbor was thinking, Hena asked does anything happen.

The neighbor said yes, a week ago the neighbor on your right had similar incident and after a week it happened to your father. I am thinking next week might be my turn.

It was night and Hena was thinking the whole night about the neighbor's "saying. In the morning Hena and the neighbor both went to the police station and told the story to the officer. Then they made a plan.

A week passed, everyone was at Hena's house and the police officer stayed at the neighbor's house. The officers were in the living room suddenly someone throw a stone to the window. Two officers got to the window and the criminal shot one of the officers, the other officer wanted to shoot the criminal but he missed his shot. But the third officer shot the criminal and the criminal got injured.

Police captured the criminal and when he became conscious from the injury they took him to the questioning room. The police asked: why did you do this, the criminal did not answer. Police asked again: why did you do this, the criminal did not answer.

Finally the criminal start talking and said I am forced to do so, if I say anything they will kill me. The police said who is gonna kill you: the criminal I can't tell you that.

Police: if you want to be a freeman and be safe then you must tell us. Criminal: they are three people forcing me to do these dirty work for them and shared the other criminals addresses with the officer as well his own address.

The police released the injured criminal and drove to the addresses the criminal shared with them.

When the police got there all three families had the same response, they are not alive (first one was killed 3 months ago, the second 2 months ago and the third one a month ago).

The officer asked the wife of the guy who was killed three months ago: how was your husband killed? The wife said my husband only wanted to write a book and he completed the book and printed it. One day he was standing in front of our house, someone shot him. I don't know why would someone kill him, he never harmed anyone.

Wife of the guy who was killed two months ago said: My husband and his friend who has been killed a month ago were investigate the matter of the book writer's case. They had found a proof and that caused him his life.

Wife of the third guy said: My husband had found several proofs on the killer and wanted to share and handover all to the police.

But someone kill him on his way to the police station and took all the proofs. I have a photo of the person who has killed my husband, when the police saw the photo the realized they have been fooled by the criminal they had released.

The officers got a call and were told the injured criminal and all his family is dead. The police quickly got to the incident location and started their investigation.

Police found that: when the criminal got to his home he wanted to escape. His wife stopped him; the criminal got mad and killed all his kids. The wife could not control and shot the criminal and due to fear of going to jail she then killed herself.

After the doctor's report the police found the criminal was addict person and then reached to Hena and his father that they are safe now.

Hena became very happy and thanked the police officer.

Chapter 3

A year passed Hena and Husain completed their college. Hena was going to Kabul for a job and told Husain she is going to Kabul.

Husain asked why! Hena I can't share that, you may understand me. Husain, I am also going to come with you. Hena, no not possible you should take care of my father. After some days Hena had her flight, Hena departed to Afghanistan and started her job.

After some days Husain called Hena and said your father is very sick and want to see you. Hena got leave and return to US, when Hena's father saw her, he got very happy and wanted to say something but unfortunately he died.

Two weeks passed Hena and Husain were chatting. Husain asked why don't you work here. Hena said I am willing to help my country, Husain I also want to come with you. I want to be a spy, Hena: can I tell you what my job is? Husain: yes anytime, whatever you want you can share with me.

Hena said I am a secret officer. Hena and Husain both went to Afghanistan. Both were working together and no one knew about them. They were successful in their work. Dangerous people were being killed every day. People would get the news from TV and newspapers. Reporters would reach the police department and ask. Is anyone been found doing all these dangerous work?

Police said I can't say a lot but we have someone, who is doing all this for their country. One day Hena was walking alongside a school and saw a small girl sitting there. Two people showed up and were kidnaping her, the small girl was yelling for help. Hena said Stop they got the girl in a vehicle and escaped. Hena could not get them but could note the Tag number of the vehicle. Hena met with her superior and discussed all the story. He said you are the strongest among us and you are authorized whatever you want to do I count on you. Hena thanked her superior and went to meet Husain. Once Husain heard the whole story, Husain said: let's check the security cameras. After checking the Security cameras they found those people had kidnaped many kids. They followed the tracks and finally Hena was able to find the vehicle she had noted the Tags. But with too much struggle. The vehicle was empty and no one was inside it, except some blood signs, so Hena and Husain followed the blood signs. Following the blood signs they reached to the main road but afterwards did not see any further blood. Hena and Husain once again checked the security cameras. They noticed the kidnappers had been to a house. So, they both been to that house and didn't found anyone except lots of blood and a phone. Hena checked all the numbers on the phone and showed one number to Husain and said this is one of our office numbers, actually one of the officers.

Hena and Husain chatted for few minutes and then draw their plan. Husain who was a spy changed his getup and waiting in that same house and Hena went to meet her boss.

She told her boss that we have found the place where the kidnappers kept the kids, but no one was there and whole place was bloody. I found a mobile phone and it had one of our staff members number on it and I think someone is playing us.

The boss quickly grabbed the phone from Hena's hand and said you are mistaken. Hena said no I am sure someone here is playing us.

The boss: If you are that much confident, find evidence which will make me confident as well. Hena: Ok and left the room, then called Husain and asked. Did anyone show up? Husain: No.

Hena, wanted to say stay there and don't go anywhere. But Husain ended the call. Husain texted a message to Hena "Don't call me they came in". The kidnappers enter the room and with them a girl entered as well. Husain was thinking the girl might be their boss and he came in front of the girl.

The girl asked: Who are you and what are you doing here?

Husain: I am also like you and I was looking to find such people until found you guys, so I can work with you. The girl: How can I trust you. Husain: I don't have anything to hide and say lie. The girl: ordered her people to take Husain away. Husain: You can't take me away like this, I am the person you guys need and can't find anyone like me.

Whatever you say I can do that, even that your people can't do it for you.

The girl: said to her men stop and told Husain Ok I was in need of someone like you., but you have to proof yourself.

At night Husain text Hena. Things are going well and nobody doubted us. At the meantime one the girl's men saw Husain and reported to the girl. Girl's men wanted to check Husain but the girl said no I am going to see him.

The girl: who are you talking to? Husain: With one of my friends. I asked her for help, she is in the business around 10 years, but she rejected.

Husain: Anyway, what are you doing here? The girl: nothing I saw your and came here. Husain: Why you are doing all this? The girl: this is the first time someone is asking me this question.

When I was a little, my mother died and my father was working in a company, after few days he lost his job. My father due to losing his job and my mother, he started doing this and taught me as well. Because of my father I am here and doing all this.

Husain: In my opinion you are a different person and introduced himself. Husain: no one would know me this quick though. The girl: I am Sara and people know me by the name of King. A few days passed and King's confidence in Husain was increasing. One day King told Husain, you should go with my men and kidnap some kids with them. Husain had recorded King's voice and sent it to Hena.

Husain went with King's men to kidnap a kid. When they kidnapped the child they saw a police vehicle and the police was following them, but Husain was able to trick the police and escape from there.

They got back to their location safely with the child. King's men wanted to tell the whole story but King said I want to hear from Husain.

Husain tell the whole story and said we couldn't do anything. But one of King's men said if it wouldn't be Husain we all would be captured by the police.

King: very well now we have someone and King told all her men to be ready. Kings men took their knives and tied kid hands and feet.

In a room was a big table and they put the girl on that table? Kings men wanted to kill the kid.

 Husain said don't kill this kid. She is too young and her organs will not benefit us.

King: Don't you also kill the kids? Husain: No, we didn't kill the kids. We were selling the kids and there was someone who would buy them.

King: Who is this person you are talking about?

Husain: This guy is buying the kids and paying lots of money.

King listened to Husain and said, bring me this guy here and we will sell the kid.

Husain went and brought Hena with him to get the kid. Hena saw the King, paid the money and got the kid. Hena returned the kid back to their family and said don't leave the kids alone.

Over the night everyone got to their beds, Husain was in a separate room and thought everyone is asleep but King was awake. Husain called Hena and was talking about their next plan.

King was listening to Husain and heard all what Husain said. King didn't know whom Husain is talking to and Husain at the end of his call said good bye Madam Police before anyone may hear us and Husain powered off his phone.

King entered the room, Husain: you are awake,

King I just come from outside, who you were taking to? Husain did you hear us? King: No, what did you guys say? Husain Oh its noting, it was my friend, who we sold the girl, I was talking to her, Well it's noting important. King, Ok and good night.

The night passed and in the morning King saw Husain going out. King ordered one of her men to follow Husain.

After two hours King's man returned and said Husain met with the person who bought the girl from us yesterday.

King realized Husain met with the Police and then King called her father and tell him everything. King's father said find me the photo of this Police. Next day Husain went out and met with Hena again. King's men were following him and they captured Hena's photos and then King send those photos to her father.

When King's father saw the photos said don't worry nothing important they can't do anything. King why they can't do anything they are the Police and not you. Kings Father my daughter don't be afraid they can't do anything, just follow my orders.

The next day Hena met with her boss and said after few days I will find the kidnappers and the person who is working with them.

Boss leave them we can't fight them, I have something else for you.

Hena how can you say like that? You are a police and Police would do anything for their country. I will do the next assignment but once I am done with the current one. I don't wanna leave my assignment in mid. You don't have to wait long, within couple of days I will capture them and the person who deceives us. Hena wanted to leave the room. Boss wait, I did give you the chance to save your friend's life and your job, but seems you don't want to. Hena, what are you talking about. Which friend and what job? Boss the one you sent to spy on my daughter. Hena what do you mean by my daughter? I don't even know your daughter. Boss for sure you know the one you bought the kid from. Boss showed Husain to Hena.

Hena saw Husain tied and his eyes were tied by a piece of cloth so he could not see anything. Boss if you want your friend to be alive you have to resign from your post.

Hena didn't have any other option and wrote her resignation. Hena I have resigned from my post and you have to release Husain right away.

Boss there is a forest close by and we will release your friend there. Hena I hope you may not cheat me this time. Hena followed the way to the forest and found Husain in the forest.

Hena What happened Husain? Husain, I don't remember very much, after we met I returned to King's place and then don't remember what happened until now. Hena its Ok they found out about our plan and King's father was my boss. They were about to kill and to save you I had to resign and I couldn't lose you. They think there is no one who can stop them. Husain now that you resigned what do you wanna do? Hena shared her new plan with Husain. Husain people should be afraid of you. Another day passed and in the morning Hena called one of her friends, who was also a police, but not a secret police. Hena told him all what happened and as well shared her new plan. Hena's friend agreed with her on the plan and agreed to help Hena. Hena was very happy and told Husain, that her friend will be helping them.

Husain: who is this friend of yours? Hena: That guy is also a Police, and he struggled a lot to become a police and my friend's name is Yahiya. Husain: I am counting the moments to see your friend. It was night and Husain was asleep, Hena left the house and went to the place where King would take kidnapped children. Hena noticed they are all still there and have not moved from that place. In the morning at 10am Hena met his friend Yahiya and told him King has not been moved from their place.

Yahiya: If they are still there we can easily capture them. Hurry, I will notify the other police and before they may move from there we should capture them. They reached to King's Place there was no one and the house was empty, the other police also arrived. They all hide around inside and outside the house. Hena and Yahiya also hide, but Husain didn't hide and waited with the Gate until King Came.

King and her father and all her men came along some kids they had kidnapped. The kids were yelling and crying but King shut their mouths. King saw Husain and said what are you doing here. No one is gonna save you this time.

King ordered her men to capture Husain. Husain: wait I have been waiting for you since morning, I am not here that you guys to kill me. We are here to free people from you and your madness.

King: what do you mean by we? Husain, you will find out and said everyone come out all. Everyone showed up except for Hena. When Yahiya showed up a kid wanted to go to him but King's father didn't let the kid to go.

Yahiya: release all the kids. Kings father: why didn't you hear their voice yet. You came for help and don't want to hear their voice. They opened the kids mouth. The kids wanted to go to Yahiya started yelling father, father.

King: now I realized why you wanted to save the kids. King's father held the kid tight and said if you want to save your child you have to work with us and be one of us.

Yahiya: I am not one of you guys, release the kids, otherwise!

King's father: otherwise what? You chose your way and chose to kill both yourself and your son.

Yahiya: Ok we will leave if you release all the kids.

King's father: what you wanna do with all kids, take your son and go with all your men.

Yahiya: I said all the kids, did you hear that?

King's father: Ok why you are so angry!

The Police officers were to leave, suddenly Yahiya said very loudly! Hena now?

King's mean had not released the kids yet. The Police who were hidden inside the house came out and arrested all King's men. Hena was also hidden inside the house, came out and said Hello my boss and arrested her boss. All were arrested except King and King wanted to escape but Husain came in front of her and said you wanted to kill me, but now you are trapped. The police arrested King as well.

Yahiya took all the children to their families and returned to Hena. Yahiya: Thanks for saving all the children; I didn't say this because of my son, but for all the children you saved and thanks a lot. If it wasn't you, now we would not have all these kids.

Hena: No need to thank me, we did it with the help of each other. If we all help together our country will soon be stable.

Husain: Hena you still want to be a secret service?

Hena: yes very much, this is what I want the most to do.

Yahiya: why you want to be a police.

Hena: Do you know friends? In this world everywhere and all the time, there are people needs help. We always expect others to help us. We have lots of police who in danger their life for others. But, we need people who will fight for this goal. If we don't do our best for the needy then who will do it.

I love my people and I am always ready to help people.

This was the day Hena thought and said to Husain and Yahiya!

The day I had accident, it changed my whole life. Just one day changed my whole life.

By Rabia Ahmadzai

8th grader Arundel Middle School year 2021-2022

RBA